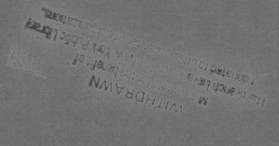

AILEEN FISHER
Know What I Saw?

ILLUSTRATED BY DEBORAH DURLAND DeSAIX

A Neal Porter Book
ROARING BROOK PRESS
New Milford, Connecticut

To George, with all my heart
—DDD

Text copyright © 2004 by Aileen Fisher
Illustrations copyright © 2005 by Deborah Durland DeSaix
A Neal Porter Book
Published by Roaring Brook Press
Roaring Brook Press is a division of Holtzbrinck Publishing Holdings Limited Partnership
143 West Street, New Milford, Connecticut 06776

Distributed in Canada by H. B. Fenn and Company Ltd.

Library of Congress Cataloging-in-Publication Data
Fisher, Aileen.
Know what I saw? / Aileen Fisher ; illustrated by Deborah Durland DeSaix.
p. cm.
"A Neal Porter Book."
Summary: A child discovers different baby animals in groups of ten to one.
ISBN 1-59643-055-9
[1. Animals—Infancy—Fiction. 2. Counting. 3. Stories in rhyme.]   I. DeSaix, Deborah Durland, ill.   II. Title.
PZ8.3.F634Kn 2005   [E]—dc22   2004024447

Roaring Brook Press books are available for special promotions and premiums.
For details contact: Director of Special Markets, Holtzbrinck Publishers.

First edition August 2005
Book design by Jennifer Browne
Printed in China
2   4   6   8   10   9   7   5   3   1

Know what I saw

in a sprawly heap?

10 little collies,
and all asleep
with legs and noses
in comical poses.
I took a picture
of them, to keep.

Know what I saw
on a farm near town?

9 baby chicks
wearing pillow down.
I thought they'd smother
beneath their mother
who looked so squatty
and wide and brown.

Know what we found
when Sheri's pup
scratched out a nest
like an old grass cup?

8 little deer mice,
eight full-of-fear mice.
Hearing them squeak,
we covered them up.

Know what I watched

when I played with Kevin?

A basketful of kittens
from one to 7—
with soft fur suits
and mittens and boots
and every one
like a gift from heaven.

Know what we saw
near a brambly rose?

That I wouldn't be lonely
if only . . . if only
I had 1 puppy
to call my own,
a pert little puppy
to call MY OWN.